THE
KING'S SINGERS'
FOLK SONGS

British folk songs
arranged for mixed voices

FABER MUSIC
in association with
FABER & FABER
Hinshaw Music Inc.

SOLE CANADIAN SELLING AGENTS
Boosey and Hawkes
(CANADA) LTD
279 YORKLAND BLVD, WILLOWDALE, ONT. M2J 1S7

First published in 1985 by Faber Music Ltd
in association with Faber & Faber Ltd
3 Queen Square London WC1N 3AU
Music drawn by Michael Langham Rowe
Printed in England by the Thetford Press

The folk songs in this collection have been recorded by the King's Singers
on HMV EL 2702491 (LP) HMV EL 2702494 (Cassette)

CONTENTS

INTRODUCTION

The folk songs we know in Britain today have been part of our heritage ever since simple hymn tunes were first given secular words and minstrels set out on their musical rounds. A game of Chinese Whispers played over the centuries gradually developed ever widening regional varieties of text and melody until the early part of this century when folk song collectors notated a wealth of beautiful material and saved the folk song tradition from being engulfed in a tide of more commercial popular music.

The King's Singers have recorded albums containing German, Austrian, French, Spanish, American and even Japanese folk songs, but here at last we return to our own islands. Our selection was guided by no more erudite consideration than that of presenting an interesting and varied collection of songs while giving free rein to our arrangers' imagination. The songs span a wide range of human emotions and are presented in a variety of styles with, we hope, something for everyone.

To preserve the sonorities inherent in the keys chosen by our arrangers, we decided with only one exception against any transpositions, and, apart from a little judicious re-scoring, these arrangements remain exactly as written for us. Instead of recommending any specific distribution of voices, we have merely indicated the range of each part, believing that the arrangements will adapt equally well to mixed and male-voice ensembles (male altos permitting!)

We make no special claims as to the authenticity of the texts choosing rather to select versions which seemed to suit a group consisting of 2 Londoners, 2 Scots, a Wessexman and an East Anglian with a Welsh-speaking wife.

The King's Singers 1985

LAMORNA

Trad. English arr. Goff Richards

6

7

10

[1] 'donnah' – dialect word meaning 'wife'.

BOBBY SHAFTOE

Trad. English arr. Gordon Langford

22

DANCE TO THY DADDY

Words by William Watson (c.1796–1840)

Trad. English arr. Goff Richards

28

O MY LOVE IS LIKE A RED, RED ROSE

Words by Robert Burns (1759-1796)

Trad. Scottish arr. Simon Carrington

38

LONDONDERRY AIR

Trad. Irish arr. Peter Knight

41

42

grave____ will war - mer, swee - ter be,____ For you will bend and tell me that you

grave____ will war - mer, swee - ter be,____ For you will bend and tell me that you

grave____ will war - mer, swee - ter be,____ For you will bend and tell me that you

love_ me,____ sleep in peace un - til you come to me.

love____ me,____ And I shall sleep in peace un - til you come to me.

love_ me,____ And I shall sleep in peace un - til you come to me.

BARBARA ALLEN

Trad. English arr. John Rutter

48

EARLY ONE MORNING

Trad. English arr. Jeremy Jackman

53

MIGILDI MAGILDI [1]

Trad. Welsh arr. Grayston Ives

1. pronounced Miggle-dee, Maggle-dee

58

63

SHE MOVED THROUGH THE FAIR

Trad. Irish arr. Daryl Runswick

THE OAK AND THE ASH

Trad. English arr. Gordon Langford

72

73

74

Oak and the Ash and the bon-ny I-vy tree, They flour-ish at home in my own coun-try."

Mm

How I wish once a-gain in the North I could be.

(niente)

NAE LUCK ABOUT THE HOUSE[1.]

Trad. Scottish arr. Gordon Langford

1. pronounced with a Scottish accent 'aboot the hoose'

© 1985 by Faber Music Limited

78

86

NAE LUCK ABOUT THE HOUSE

Glossary

aboon	-	above
bauk	-	A tie beam of a house, stretching from wall to wall. In old one-storey houses these were often exposed and used for hanging or placing articles on
blawn by	-	blown by
braw	-	brave, splendid, fine
caller	-	fresh
cauld	-	cold
fling by	-	cast aside hastily
gar	-	to make, to cause, to do
ilka	-	same, identical, the very same
lave	-	the rest
mair	-	more
muckle	-	big, great
neist	-	next
straw	-	to scatter about, spread loosely